Made possible

by a donation

from the

Thomas M. Kirbo & Irene B. Kirbo
Charitable Trust

1995

Hippo's *Adventure*

in Alphabet Town

*written and illustrated
by Janet McDonnell*

created by Wing Park Publishers

 CHILDRENS PRESS ®

CHICAGO

Library of Congress Cataloging-in-Publication Data

McDonnell, Janet, 1962-
    Hippo's adventure in Alphabet Town / written and illustrated by
Janet McDonnell.
        p.   cm. — (Read around Alphabet Town)
    Summary: Hippo meets "h" words on his adventure in
Alphabet Town. Includes activities.
    ISBN 0-516-05408-2
    [1. Alphabet—Fiction.   2. Hippopotamus—Fiction.]   I. Title
II. Series.
PZ7.M478436Hk   1992
[E]—dc 20   91-20549
                                                                      CIP
                                                                       AC

Hippo's *Adventure*

in Alphabet Town

You are now entering Alphabet Town,
With houses from "A" to "Z."
I'm going on an "H" adventure today,
So come along with me.

This is the "H" house of Alphabet Town. A huge hippo lives here.

Hippo loves ''h'' things. His house
is filled with them.

Hippo loves Halloween. It is
his favorite holiday. Can you
guess why?

And Hippo loves playing hide-and-seek.

But most of all, Hippo likes to play hopscotch with his friend,

Hog.

One day while they were playing,
Hippo started to hiccup. "Oh, no,"
said Hippo. "I have the hiccups."

"Hold your breath," said Hog. "That will stop your hiccups." So Hippo held his breath. "How do you feel?" asked Hog.

"HICCUP!" said Hippo.

Hippo's hiccup was so loud that

Hen

came running to see what happened.
"Maybe Hen can help," said Hog.
"I hope so," said Hippo.

"We need to scare Hippo," said Hen.
"That will stop his hiccups. I know
just what to do. Meet me on H Street
in one hour."

In one hour, Hippo and Hog met
Hen on H Street. "Welcome to the

haunted house,"

said Hen. "Come with me."

Hippo walked down the hall of the
haunted house. Just then, out jumped
a huge ghost! "Boo!" hollered the
ghost.

"Hello, Horse," said Hippo. "Hiccup." Hog and Hen just looked at each other.

"I do not think we can help
your hiccups," said Hen.

"Maybe we should take you to the hospital,"

said Horse.

"The hospital!" said Hippo. "But I am a healthy hippo. I just have the hiccups."

"Maybe you need rest," said Hog.
"Why don't you hop into your

and take a nap?"
"I will," said Hippo. "Hiccup."

And with that, Hippo hopped into his hammock.

But the hammock flipped over.
Hippo hit the ground.

"Hippo! Hippo!" cried Hog, Hen, and Horse. "Are you hurt?"

But Hippo was not hurt. He was laughing hard. "Hee, hee, ho, ha, ha," he laughed.

He laughed so hard, guess what happened. "My hiccups are gone!" said Hippo.

"Hurray!" said Hippo's friends.
They gave Hippo a big hug.
Then guess what happened.

"Hiccup!" said Horse.
"Oh, no," said Hippo, Hog, and
Hen. "Here we go again."

MORE FUN WITH HIPPO

What's in a Name?

In my "h" adventure, you read many "h" words. My name begins with an "H." Many of my friends' names begin with "H" too. Here are a few.

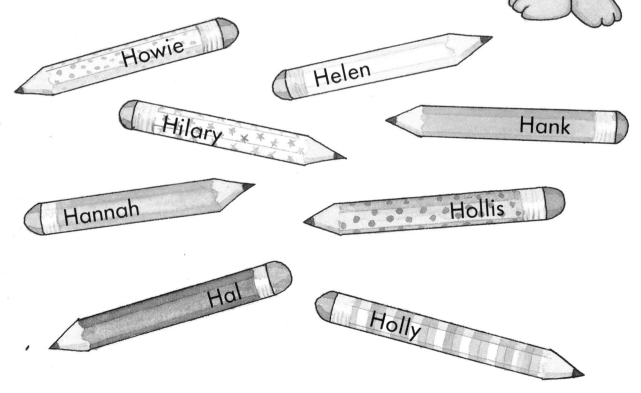

Do you know other names that start with "H"?
Does your name start with "H"?

Hippo's Word Hunt

I like to hunt for words with "h" in them. Can you help me find the words on this page that begin with "h"? How many are there? Can you read the words?

pitcher

cake

hand

moth

hat

fish

mother

Can you find any words with "h" in the middle?
Can you find any words with "h" at the end?
Can you find a word with no "h"?

Hippo's Favorite Things

"H" is my favorite letter. I love
"h" things. Can you guess why?
You can find some of my favorite
"h" things in my house on page 7.
How many "h" things can you
find there? Can you think of
more "h" things?

Now you make up an "h" adventure.